MW01010283

Hunter Blue Hyatt

This book is dedicated to my beautiful children Anala and Desmond Jr, my nieces, nephews and all the little minds with big ideas.

IT'S OK TO BE ANGRY

Co-Authors:

Alana Atkins-Jamison &

Anala Jamison

Hi, my name is Nally and I'm 4 years old. I am smart and energetic! My mommy and daddy always teach me new things because I really like learning. We do a lot of cool things together! I love being happy and bringing joy to others, but sometimes I feel angry.

I love doing origami (that's a fancy word for paper folding). My favorite thing to make is an airplane. Look at this one. It's SUPER cool and it's gunna fly high in the sky.

Nally throws the paper plane and quickly it falls to the ground.

"Uh oh. I know, I will try again."

She throws it once more a bit harder, but it falls to the floor again.

Determined, Nally says, "Ok... ok, it will work for sure this time!"

She pulls her arm back as hard as she can and throws the airplane with all her might. It goes up high and quickly falls to the ground. Nally grabs the plane and crumples it. "I'm feeling a little angry," she mumbles.

She walks away from the crumpled plane, toward the table and notices a puzzle her mom laid out.

"I'm sure I can do this by myself," Nally thinks. She takes a seat at the table and starts working on the puzzle.

"This is easy!" she boasts, but as she continues to work, the puzzle gets more difficult.

"Where does this piece go? It's not fitting anywhere! I'm feeling angry."

   As she throws the puzzle pieces down, her mom yells from the kitchen, "Can you help your baby brother with his bottle honey?"

   She replies, "Sure mommy!" and thinks to herself, "I'm absolutely sure I can do this!"

She proudly struts over to her baby brother and holds his bottle up. "Oh, not like that baby, you're holding the bottle much too low for him to drink," her mom explains.

"I CAN'T DO ANYTHING RIGHT!" Nally screams as she runs to her room.

Her mom goes to check on the baby. She notices the crumpled airplane on the floor and incomplete puzzle on the table. She then follows after Nally.

Hey, what's going on honey?" her mother asks. "I couldn't fly my paper airplane; I couldn't finish the puzzle and didn't feed my brother right. I'M SO ANGRY!!!" Nally shouts.

"It's ok to be angry," her mom reassures her. "We have so many emotions inside of us and anger is one of them. Everything shouldn't make us angry, but some things will. It's ok to express your anger, but it's not ok to scream, throw things or leave them in the floor because you're upset. You won't always be happy, and that's ok, but you still have to behave appropriately."

Her mom continues, "when you are angry, it is important to control your mind or you won't be able to see things clearly. When you don't control your thoughts, you can't control your body."

"Then what can I do when I'm angry?" Nally asks.

"Well, you can talk about it or write down how you feel. You can count to 10 or ask for some time to yourself..."

"Or jump on my trampoline?" Nally interrupts excitedly.

"You sure can!" her mom replies. "But always remember, anger is only temporary, and it takes a really brave person to ask for help."

"It does?" Nally asks.

"Absolutely! You remember our daily affirmation, don't you?" her mom responds.

"Oh yeah!" as she begins to proudly recite:

"I'm not perfect, but I'm perfectly me and I strive to be my best daily.

I am brave.
I am brilliant.
I am beautiful.
I am powerful.
I am chosen."

"That's right! You DEFINITELY are! Always remember that." her mom says as she picks her up and spins her around.

"Now go uncrumple your airplane and pick up those puzzle pieces so we can work on them TOGETHER!"

What do you do when you're angry?

35845241R00018

Made in the USA
San Bernardino, CA
15 May 2019